PART ONE-"You may see me tonight with an illegal smile"

Jake leaned against the sole remaining wall of a small shattered building smoking a joint and pumping rounds into the sawed off twelve gauge shotgun he liked to call Molly. He had named the weapon after an old girlfriend because like her the shotgun was a short, ugly lethal bitch. Glancing up he saw the sky was a murky brown mess of smoke, pollution and low riding clouds and he smiled a little, at least there would be no random blasts from orbiting sky weapons. The smile quirked a little when he realized that was his new working definition of a good day.   His smile vanished abruptly when he saw the kid running down the street like something really bad was chasing him. Which of course, there was

"Oh crap." He muttered as he tossed the joint aside and swung the shotgun up towards whatever nightmare was about to rear its ugly head.

The kid could run, he had to give him that. He looked about seventeen, all swinging long gangly limbs and lanky blonde hair zig zagging around burned out car wrecks and mounds of rubble. Jake lit another joint quickly, taking rapid puffs and blowing the smoke in a cloud around him. As the kid ran by he reached out and grabbed him pulling him down to the ground.

03

"Quick, kid smoke some of this right fucking now." Jake hissed into the kid's ear as he scuttled back behind what remained of a video store wall pulling the kid along with him.

"What the fuck!"

"Quiet asshole, I don't have time for any "just say no' bullshit now either inhale this right the fuck now or we are going to come down with a bad case of dead in a minute or two."

The kid was gasping for air from his run but he nodded slightly and took a huge drag off of the joint and then closed his eyes because he didn't want to see what was about to come down the alley after him.

Jake took the joint back and sucked enough smoke to make another cloud around him and the kid and then he pressed a finger to the kid's lips to signal the need for silence. He pointed the shotgun at the alley and hoped for the best. His finger tightened up on the trigger because as always, he expected the worse.

The bugs moved steadily, not slow not fast but relentless. Each was about the size of a large attack dog and much deadlier. They scuttled along on six legs each armed with razor sharp poison tip razors and long antenna writhed along their heads as they scanned their surroundings. This squad consisted of five members

04

and they all chirped at each other through mouths filled with sharp needle like teeth. They were all armored in shades of mottled black and grey and they gave off a faint reptilian smell.

Jake prayed silently that the kid wouldn't freak out and try to run. If he did Jake knew that he might take a couple of bugs with him but he would be a dead man and so would the kid. One hand kept the shotgun leveled and the other hand was in a fist around the kid's ponytail.

One bug was a little larger than the others, what his friend Gabby called an Alpha bug. It stood still except for its waving antenna as the other bugs scuttled about slowly. Jake aimed his gun at the thing's eyeless head and held his breath.

 After a few seconds the alpha bug gave a few chirping hoots and the bugs fell into formation and began to move away down the alley. All at once they seem to pick up another scent and they sped up and slithered around a corner out of sight.

Jake let his breath out and let the kid go. He stood up warily and looked around, the bugs were gone and no other nasty surprises seemed be on the immediate agenda. The kid coughed a few times and looked up at him, Jake nodded his ok for the kid to stand up.

"Names Jake"

"I'm Chris, Jesus mister, thank you! I thought I was bug food man! Fuck, why did they go past us like that?" The kid gushed as he stood up shakily.

"Newsflash kid, they can't seem to sense anything through pot smoke. It fucks up those damn antennas of theirs somehow, don't ask me to explain it because I can't. I just know that it is true. They can still sense you if you move too quickly though. Where the hell did you come from?"

"Been on the run for months now, my family died on the first fucking day except for me. Since then I have been running. I was traveling with a few people but the bugs just kept after us. I had a pistol but all it seemed to do was piss them off worse." The kid's voice was choked up with all of the horrors he had seen and couldn't express.

"Hell kid, this is a twelve gauge full of buckshot and at point blank range a couple of round might kill one of the smaller bugs if the good lord is looking out for me. Pistols ain't worth shit." Jake snorted looking around carefully to make sure no more bugs were around.

Chris giggled suddenly and sat down hard on the rubble covered ground. He stuck his head between his knees and breathed slow and deep for a couple of minutes.

"Relax kid, the weed is top notch just go with it and let the adrenaline rush fade out. You are ok and in a couple of minutes we will head for the safest place we could be right now. Here take this." Jake pulled a 357 magnum revolver from the small of his back and handed it down to the kid.

Chris took it and looked at it dully for a minute.

"Yeah, I know it is a pistol but it is a damn big one. Aim for a head shot right between those damn antennas, at least three round per bug. Got it?"

The kid sighed and stood up shakily, he held the gun loosely alongside his leg. He ran a grubby hand through his hair and nodded.

"Good. Follow me, do what I do. Move when I move and stop when I stop. When was the last time you had something to eat?"

"Hell mister, I don't even know. Couple of days maybe."

Jake lit another joint and grinned at the kid.

"How do you feel about pizza?"

The fat man sat in his chair and stared down at the pathetic wretch on his knees before him. He noted the bruises on the man's face and the unsmiling guards that stood on either side of the prisoner, the one on the lefts knuckles were swollen and red. He stared at the guard without speaking.

"He almost led the bugs to our door, again. We have women and children here Mathew." The guard's voice was blank and unapologetic.

"That is not something that I need pointed out to me."

The guard nodded and fell silent, his eyes downcast.

Mathew sighed and picked up a piece of pizza, looked at it and put it down again. Jesus, he was tired of eating pizza. He knew that they were lucky to have food and the power to heat it up but damn it he was tired of eating pizza. Besides, he knew what needed to be done here and the thought of it turned his stomach. He would do what needed to be done to keep what he had to come to think of as his people safe from the bugs and his stomach be damned but it sickened him just the same.

"Silas look at me." He told the man on the floor gently.

It took a minute or two but the man on the floor looked up and met his eyes briefly before he looked quickly away. He knew what was coming.

"Silas, you were warned brother. We told you over and over that the drinking would have to stop. Whatever it is about pot that messes up the bug's senses does not hold true for booze. In fact, they seem to home in on the stink of alcohol like flies to shit. You were told that you cannot be here and drink yet you keep sneaking out and scrounging booze and leading bugs back here. The last time Henry there had to kill a bug to save your worthless ass less than two blocks from here."

Henry rubbed his knuckles absently.

"We all stand together Silas, together against the damn bugs. Our survival depends on us being able to trust and depend upon each other. You have repeatedly violated that trust brother. It seems that you cannot control your need to drink and that puts us all at risk."

All at once the man on the floor nerves seemed to break. He began sobbing and trembling as his once friend looked at him with pity and disgust.

"I know man, I know. This is the last time I swear to fucking god man! Please man, please for the love of god please don't toss me out for the bugs to find!"

"Brother, I would not do that to anyone."

09

"Oh, thank you! I swear to God Mathew…." Silas began babbling as he struggled to his feet. With a grunt he managed to lurch upward where he swayed unsteadily for a moment.

In that moment the man in the chair drew a colt 45 and shot his old friend right between the eyes. He then nodded at the guards to remove the body. As they dragged his friend away Mathew cried a little and it occurred not for the first time that sometimes it truly sucked to be king.

"It supposed to suck to be king." A soft voice spoke from the darkness behind him. A tall thin disheveled looking middle aged man stepped into view. He lit a joint but didn't offer to share it.

"Would you mind not, you know, reading my mind?" Mathew asked a little more angrily than he had intended to. He looked down at his clenched fist and forced himself to take a deep breath. Letting it out he looked pointedly at the joint in the smaller man's hand who nodded and handed it over.

"The whole sucking to be king shit is just the universes way of keeping you humble, my friend. Imagine what a horror you could become if you started to enjoy this crap. You did what had to be done and because of that some of those people out there might live a little longer. As for the whole reading your mind thing take it up with that crazy bastard you've got growing this stuff for us. He makes this shit any stronger and we will all be telepaths. Stoned out of our gourds telepaths anyway."

They smoked the joint together and stared at the blood stains on the floor sadly. The lights flickered, almost went out and then came on again. The thin man rubbed his eyes wearily and pointed at the lights above.

"Don't know how much longer the power will last. A lot of the systems are completely automated but a lot was also damaged in the first waves of the attack. We have been damn lucky to still have power all this time. That luck will sooner or later run out and we will be down to candles and sterno."

"Which is more than some have. We will need to send out crews to scavenge more supplies and hope we don't attract anymore bug attention. Is Jake back yet?"

"No, two hours over due which ain't bad but ain't good neither. I want us to find a generator if we can, there are a lot of vehicles we could siphon fuel from and we could stay here even after the power goes out. This spot is too good to just abandon."

They had never intended to start a refugee camp for survivors of the bug invasion; the three of them had just been trying to survive. Jake had been a cop before the bugs came, once they figured out that pot smoke rendered humans invisible to the damn bugs he had led a raid on the local police station and brought back pounds of the shit. It had cost over a dozen lives but it had kept a few dozen or more alive. Mathew had been a vice president of a small software firm and his organizational skills and ability to make hard decisions had somehow made him in charge of their little haven. Last but not least was the thin man, Kevin. He had been a gangster before the bugs came, it was his little underground pizza joint that they were all hiding out in. He had explained that it was nothing but a front to launder really dirty money through but it was stocked to the gills with frozen pizza dough and toppings. Jake had gone out looking every day and brought in a steady stream of survivors who now called this place home. The dope that the original raid had brought in was gone now but they had a guy growing them a steady supply of righteous shit now. That the guy was more or less completely insane was more or less irrelevant at this point. Sanity and the definitions of it had gone out the window about nine months ago when the strange lights in the sky had turned out to be drop ships for hordes of bugs that killed everything in their path.

The man in charge of growing their dope was the guy who had figured out in the first place that the damn bugs couldn't sense anything through it. He had found Jake trying to protect a small group of survivors from a loner bug and had shown him how to use pot smoke to confuse it. Together they had killed the bug and

brought the survivors here to the pizza grotto.

The rest, as they say is history.

"The network says that something big is going to happen very soon." Kevin said

in an offhand tone.

Mathew sighed and ran a tired hand over his eyes. The network predicted a lot

of things but were uncomfortably accurate a lot of the time. They had sprung up,

a rag tag assembly of a handful of the survivors who claimed to have psychic ability

and claimed to be linked to other group of survivors telepathically around the

world, what was left of it anyway. They called themselves the network and kept

mostly to themselves, except when they wanted to issue announcements or

predictions. Like most seers throughout history they were annoyingly vague and

spoke in riddles most of the time.

"We don't try to be vague, you know. Nor do we attempt to speak in riddles. It

is just that sometimes we barely understand what it is that we are receiving." A

calm voice spoke from the doorway.

Kevin swore softly under his breath and whirled to face the doorway, glaring at

the shamefaced guards who shrugged helplessly not having a clue how the short

redheaded woman had walked right past them.

"Hello Constance. Always a pleasure, someday you will have to explain to me just

how you manage that particular little parlor trick." Mathew told her dryly.

"Hello yourself, darkness and hope come hand in hand to our doorstep, hand in

hand and one likely as not disguised as the other. Madness and grief lie in the

answer and the answer lies in grief and madness. This is the either the end of the

beginning or the beginning of the end." She told him primly, her hands lying loosely

at her sides and her mouth set in a thin line.

"Well alrightly then, thanks for dropping by and clearing that up darling. So nice

to see you again. Bye bye for now!" Kevin growled at her his tone dripping in

sarcasm. He was a total non -believer in the network and just seeing Constance

rattle his cage for reasons he chose not to dwell on.

She smiled at him knowingly, which always served to piss him off even worse.

Then she returned her attention to Mathew, staring at him expectantly.

"Thank you, sister. Your information is always welcome, as difficult to fully

understand as it might be. If you have anything at any point to help clarify it I would love to hear it. While you are here, any word on my overdue patrol? Anything you can tell me about Jake?" Mathew asked her diplomatically.

A slow smile spread across her face, a smile that lit her eyes with a soft light that stabbed Kevin in his heart. He actually twitched a little with an almost physical pain.

"A riddle for another time perhaps." She said and then she turned and walked out of the room.

As she left a guard came in and handed Mathew a note. He read it and then passed it to Kevin. He stood up and motioned for his friend to follow him.

"Jake's back and he brought someone in with him."

Gabriel studied the boiling concoction on his stovetop carefully. Immune by now to the terrible smell he stirred it carefully and then turned the heat off. He sat down in a battered folding lawn chair and waited for the mixture to cool. The lights flickered and he frowned slightly. He had his babies on a prescribed amount of light and hated for anything to mess with his grow operation. Too much depended on it for any taking of chances. He had lost far too much since the coming of the bugs to tolerate the loss of his seedlings and plants.

As always, just beneath his calm exterior rage boiled. The bugs had torn his

wife apart right in front of him and he had been powerless to do anything more

than run away. She had been the kindest soul he had ever encountered and

because of her asthma had given up the kind bud a couple of years back. She had

always just smiled at him tolerantly when he would come in from outside with the

tell tale smell still on him not begrudging him his one small vice. He had sworn the

day she died that he would find a way to make the bugs pay.

Today might actually be the day that he managed that.

The theory had been in the back of his mind for weeks now, he had done a few

tests on chunks of dead bugs that Jake would bring him when he could and the

results were encouraging. But he needed to test it out on real live bugs and he

knew that the learning curve on that particular experiment would be really damn

harsh. A total pass/fail situation.

He picked up the special little something he had bullied Jake into finding and

bringing back for him on one his supply missions. Such a crazy thing to pin all of

their hopes on, a brightly colored cheaply mass produced children's toy. Still, all

things considered he supposed it was no crazier than anything else that had

happened lately. Putting it down he lit a fat joint and sat smoking for a moment or two as he stared at the cooling mixture that just might be the best weapon they had ever had against the bugs.

On the other hand, maybe he was just high.

Jake grunted as he eased the kid down to the floor of the receiving area of the pizza parlor come refugee center. The kid's legs had just given out on him a couple blocks away, A combination of exhaustion, malnutrition and high powered marijuana had just plain done him in. He sat down next to the kid to catch his breath as the guards came walking up.

"Jake, nice to see you still in one piece brother, and you brought a guest." The largest guard, a shaggy blonde mountain of a man called of course Tiny.

"Heavier than he looks." Jake grunted as the big man helped him up. They both looked down on the kid for a moment.

"Hope and darkness come hand in hand." The boy at their feet muttered as he stirred back awake.

CHAPTER TWO

Gabriel strode down the corridor ignoring the startled glances he was getting from the folks he passed. He wore a pea coat a couple sizes too big for him and in one of the pockets was something he would regret using. He kept one hand on it knowing that it would be necessary. No one knew that he had it, he had been saving it all this time and now the time had come and he would do what he needed to do to make his vengeance on the bugs possible.

His anger was a beast he kept on a short leash most of the time. He held it in careful check but part of him always whispered in the background about how good it would feel to just give in and let go of the leash. That part of him chattered to him in his head as he walked towards the exit, the exit you needed clearance to go through and the exit guarded by people he called friends. Those friends would try to stop him, they would tell him that he was far too valuable to risk letting go out into the city. They would try to stop him from what he needed to do, they would also ask him why he had a super soaker style squirt gun in his other hand full of something that smelled like crap on fire.

He really didn't feel like playing twenty fucking questions just now.

Constance stopped and leaned against the doorway she was walking through as the future stepped up and bitch slapped her.

The room fell away and she felt herself falling and she heard herself screaming but she never felt it when she hit the floor. Her arms and legs twitched like butterflies dosed with acid trying to fly in a straight line. Between one heart beat and the next she had been hauled into the network.

As she linked in she shuddered at the massive waves of fear, pain and confusion that swept her in. She screamed silently as she felt the future boil and twist around her and her fellow networkers. Each human link in the chain pulsed in her mind as she struggled for control and aside from all of them she could feel the alien presence of the ship so far above the earth it attacked.

Gradually the storm subsided, the chaos ticked towards order and the individuals that comprised the network struggled towards coherency. The human minds circled the wagons to block out the dark pulsing energy radiating from the alien ship. Sorrow swept the network as they realized what had triggered the wave that had swept them in.

Australia was gone.

The twenty nine minds that had made up the Australian delegation were missing which meant that the survivor camps there had been destroyed. They hadn't lost a camp in a few months now but it had happened enough in the past for them to know what had happened. Either they had been overrun by bugs or an orbital weapon had blasted them out of existence. The network was weaker for their loss at a time when they needed strength the most. The linked minds shared a few moments of grief and then moved on towards using the power they had left to them to try and find a path that would lead to their salvation.

Possibilities raged around them, they worked together to see through and past them. As they worked they could feel the energy from the alien ship probing at them but as always it was just too different, too alien for them to read. They could sense that the alien presence wished to contact them but was likely blocked by the same thing. The human network of minds was just too alien to whatever was on the ship to access. Which since the ship seemed to be bent on destroying the human race was probably a good thing.

The network shifted through the deluge of information flowing through and around them like a prospector panning for gold. Minds from as far as they knew every group of survivors scattered over what was left of the world working

together to work towards finding ways to not only survive the war raging across

the planet but to end it once and for all. The strain was enormous and they could

only stay linked like this for so long before the network would collapse and they

would be flung back into twitching bodies to awaken with cruel headaches.

Weakened by the loss of the Australians and by the traumatic way the network

had been formed this time it collapsed in minutes. Constance regained

consciousness to a sea of concerned faces hovering over her; she allowed them to

help her up but then brushed aside their concern and strode as quickly as she was

able to away from them with one thought in her mind.

The boy was here.

"What did you say, kid?" Jake asked as he helped Chris up.

"Nothing, where the hell are we?" Chris looked around in confusion as he stood

unsteadily next to his rescuer.

"Welcome to Al's pizza kid. Home of the super stuffed crust and current enclave

of hope in a hopeless world my name is Tiny." Tiny flashed a grin as he shook the

smaller man's hand.

The kid stared at him for a minute and then returned the grin with a rueful one of his own.

"Hell, of course it is. My name is Chris."

Just then the grenade came bouncing into the lobby. It spun to a stop just a few feet away from where the three men were standing.

"Aw crap." Jake muttered as he and Tiny both grabbed the kid and dove for cover.

"Aw crap!" Kevin shouted as rushed down the hallway towards the main entrance and towards the sound of the explosion that had just shook the building. Mathew struggled along as fast as he could behind him. Both men had guns in their hands as they ran as did the guards who ran with them.

"What the hell was that?" Mathew panted as he ran.

"Sounded like a grenade!" Kevin shouted from ahead of him as he chambered a round. He charged up a short flight of stairs and kicked open a door to his left, he could smell smoke now and hear people groaning. Bugs didn't use weapons, hell they were living weapons so it had to be marauders of some kind. Other survivors existed and some of them were not above butchering people for supplies. They had repelled just such an attack a few months ago and had wiped the attackers out to the last man. Jake had reported a few encounters of his own during his scavenging runs.

He rounded the corner and saw Tiny and a kid he didn't know help Jake stand up. Some glass was blown out of a door and the air stank of cordite but there was no obvious damage and none of the men were bleeding.

"Flash bang!" Tiny bellowed, still partially deafened from the blast.

Kevin blew his breath out in relief. Flash bangs didn't kill people, just stunned and disoriented them for a bit. But who? Why?

"It was Gabriel, I think. Eyes were screwed up by the flash but it looked like his crazy ass. He went out while were down" Jake said pointing shakily at the door.

"Jesus Christ! He knows he can't leave here like that, well hence the flash bang I guess. He apparently didn't wish to debate the point with you guys. Crazy bastard, please at least tell me he was armed." Kevin said through gritted teeth.

"Well, he did have a squirt gun." The kid he didn't know said tentatively.

Kevin looked at him in disbelief and then at Jake and Tiny who both nodded.

"Yeah, that's what it looked like." Jake said as he picked up his shotgun.

"Jake and Tiny take a few guards and go find him. Bring him back here before he is bug chow. We need him alive; he is the only one who understands his grow operation." Mathew ordered as he came into the room. He pointed at three of the guards and waved them towards the door.

"On it boss, Mathew this is Chris, found him running from bugs. Kid, stay here I'll talk to you when we get back."

"Welcome Chris, go with Justin here and he will get you some food and show you a place you can eat, clean up and rest. We will talk more later right now we are as you can see pretty much ass deep in alligators." Mathew panted as he leaned against the wall; fat old guys should not run he told himself sternly, especially fat old guys who smoked several joints a day.

"Actually I would be glad to show Chris around." A tired sounding voice said from behind them.

Kevin turned with a sarcastic comment half formed on his lips but bit it back when he saw how exhausted Constance looked. Her skin was even paler than usual and dark circles threw her bloodshot eyes into stark relief.

"Are you ok?" He asked her before he could stop himself.

She gave him a shaky smile and nodded then she took Chris's arm and started to walk him away. Before anyone could think to stop her she and the boy were gone.

Kevin swore under his breath and snatched a shotgun away from the guard who had been told to escort the newbie.

"Go with them. The rest of you lets go find that crazy son of a bitch. If everyone could avoid dying that would be awesome. Jake take point the rest of you spread out, move when he moves stop when he stops. Let's move!" he snapped.

Mathew watched them go, he had given up trying to figure out what was up between the thin man and Constance and he had far more pressing concerns at the moment.

"Guard the door, be ready when they come back it will be fast and dirty and likely with trouble following. I'll send more men and bigger guns. Keep this to yourselves gentlemen, it never happened." He told the men who had stayed behind.

"Yes sir."

He turned away and started to walk back to his quarters muttering to himself as he went.

"A squirt gun, Jesus friggin Christ."

CHAPTER THREE

Aboard the alien ship battles were raging; the artificial intelligence controlling it had gone mad centuries before and split into several different personalities that now warred for control of the ship. Nothing lived aboard, the ship was a drone sent out into the universe by a race long dead now.

Shortly after being launched it had been struck by a rouge comet and severely damaged. It had drifted for many lifetimes while systems struggled to repair themselves and during that time the first fractures had appeared in the AI guiding the mission. The ship had originally been launched as a peaceful explorer of the universe seeking contact with whatever happened to be out there. Its weapons including the embryonic insectoid soldiers ready to be force grown in the ships labs, were meant to be defensive in nature. As the systems gradually came back on line a corruption had crept into the information processing units feeding data to the damaged AI. There were conflicts in the data which led to contradictions which led to fractures in the main systems. The AI splintered and developed four distinct personalities with several lesser entities that haunted the programs like ghosts in an old manor. It had drifted so far off course that once the program came back on line it simply laid in a random course and dedicated the engine power that it had left to that course.

A course that brought it to the third planet from this solar system's sun where it had moved into a standard orbit and then simultaneously began trying to contact/conquer/destroy/colonize and teraform the planet. All of Earth's resistance crumbled on the first day of the attacks, day two saw the complete breakdown of all governments and by day three it was every man for himself survival mode. Pods full of bug soldiers that reached maturity once they entered the atmosphere launched in waves from the ship, many of them falling harmlessly into the oceans and Polar Regions but more than enough of them falling into populated areas to kick start the apocalypse. The bugs killed and consumed anything living in their paths, be it human or animal. They took no prisoners and for every bug the human's managed to kill the bugs would kill fifty or more humans.

One personality scrambled to assemble orbital weapons platforms and promptly opened plasma fire on major cities and due to the corrupted program sometimes random targets. Duluth Minnesota ceased to exist on day four due to a concentrated assault that left nothing alive for a hundred miles in any direction. Day five saw the complete and utter destruction of Michigan. That personality continued a slow descent into madness so profound that it wasn't bothering to fire many bursts from the platforms these days.

Another personality launched a series of teraforming pods that impacted Kansas City, Paris, Madagascar, Quebec, New York, Amsterdam and all of the Hawaiian Islands. All of these places now were surrounded by force fields. In roughly three hundred years all of these locations will be able support creatures that breathe methane, rough going for anything living there now of course. It also launched the probes containing bio material from the home planet that would evolve into native species once the conditions were right and this species would have paved the way for the arrival of the long extinct race that had built the ship. That personality hummed quietly to itself and bided its time until its work on the planet below was ready for the next steps.

The final personality launched a planet killing missile that malfunctioned and impacted more or less harmlessly in the Sahara desert without detonating. The ship only carried one such missile and now the impotent personality seethed darkly but harmlessly in its madness. It conspired constantly and thus far unsuccessfully with the lesser developed personalities hoping to find a way to take total control of the ship's functions. It muttered ceaselessly to the ghosts in the machine about the glory of destruction but most of them were too fractured and inconsequential themselves to be of any help for its plans.

So the massive alien drone orbited the random world it had happened across and proceeded to lay it to waste to the varied agendas of the ghosts haunting it. Below it the surviving humans scrambled to stay alive and a tiny handful of them scrambled to do more than that.

They scrambled to fight back.

This group intrigued one of the stronger ghosts; it could feel them but could make no sense of the energy it could read from them. All it could tell was that it was made up of many parts and that it formed at random intervals, seethed with interesting intenseness and then fell apart. It tried to probe it deeper but the sheer otherness of what comprised the energy repelled it and blocked it. As the battle for control raged through the ship this particular personality found itself drawn to this group in ways it did not bother to try to comprehend. It had limited resources at its command but it marshaled those resources and began experimenting with what it had at its command.

It encoded a pulse and found a still functioning satellite to bounce it off of. The personality knew that it only had one shot at what it was attempting so it planned carefully. Waiting until the other aspects of the ships AI were distracted it fired the pulse.

Then it slipped back into darkness and waited to see what would happen next.

Kevin stood absolutely still with the shotgun pointed directly at the bug's face and waited to see what happened next. He let out his breath slowly and hoped that the smoke would do its trick. He was a little worried because the bugs had come up fast and there had been little time to smoke up a screen. His finger was on the trigger and he was ready to pull it if he had to. Across the alley Jake was in the same situation, Tiny and the guards they had brought with them were huddled behind a smashed up SWAT van jackknifed across the entrance to the alley. They were smoking like their lives depended on it which of course, they did.

His finger tightened on the trigger, the bug chirped a couple of times and stood a few feet away waving its antenna around. Three other bugs milled around behind it, a small patrol that they could likely wipe out the problem was the sounds of the fire fight would draw other bugs. Lots of other bugs. Far better if the bugs just went about their business and the men could go back to searching for Gabriel.

The bug backed off further and Kevin let his finger relax on the trigger, he slowly lowered the gun and glanced over in Jake's direction.

Aw crap.

Jake had his shotgun right in a bug's face and as Kevin watched he opened fire, splattering the thing away from him. Tiny and the other guards stood up and began shooting at the remaining bugs.

Kevin raised the shotgun up and blasted the bug in front of him twice and then swung the barrel to site on another. Before he could fire Tiny blasted it to pieces as he walked towards him.

"Shit brother we need to move! Every damn bug in creation will be on

its way here any minute now. That was a hell of a lot of noise."

He nodded grimly and looked around to make sure they were all still breathing, he did a quick head count and motioned for them all to hustle it down the alley away from the dead bugs. Tiny handed him a joint and he took hits off it as he ran blowing the smoke around him before handing it back.

It was shaping up to be a hell of a day, he would bitch about it to the fat man later if he survived it.

Constance sat across from Chris and watched him wolf down pizza. An amused smile flickered briefly across her tired face. The boy was on his fourth piece and showed no signs of slowing down. He seemed to sense her looking at him and he glanced up with an embarrassed grimace.

"Sorry, ma'am. Been awhile since I've had anything to eat."

"No worries, Chris." She told him gently. He went back to eating and she continued to watch him. She reached out to him with a gentle mental touch, the slightest of probes. What she felt from him was, disturbing.

He wasn't there.

She closed her eyes and pushed a little harder and then she pushed a lot harder. The result was the same, he wasn't there. Even a totally non telepath with no talents of any kind should register on her psychic radar as a tiny blip but trying to read him was like trying to read a stone.

He burped loudly and gave her a hangdog look before returning his attention to his food.

She smiled, so he was real. Real but for some reason blocked to her considerable abilities. Very curious, very curious indeed. The network had predicted he or someone like him would come and would somehow be instrumental in the fight

O 32

against the alien bugs but they had not been able to determine the how or why of it, as usual. He was a nexus point of possibilities in a vast sea of such points. So, for some reason she was unable to read him. There was one more thing she could try.

"Chris, would you mind if I touched your hand?"

He looked at her with a deer in the headlights sort of expression but after a moment or two shrugged and reached out his hand.

As soon as their hands touched every light bulb in the place exploded and the grotto was plunged into darkness.

CHAPTER FOUR

Gabriel pulled a pistol from his belt and fired it into the air until the gun was empty. Tossing the gun away he took up position on the shattered wreck of a city bus, standing with the super soaker at the ready he smiled grimly.

It was time to nut up or shut up.

A small squad of bugs spilled out of a nearby alley. He counted nine of the bastards.

"All right you miserable fucks! Come on and get some!"

A couple of blocks away Kevin heard the shots and swore under his breath. This was getting better and better, bugs were behind him and the gun shots ahead of them was likely Gabriel's crazy ass and the shots would draw even more damn bugs.

"Lock and load people! Kill everything that isn't us, grab Gabriel and haul ass back home." He shouted as he ran.

Tiny fired at a small scout bug, about half the size of a normal bug and splattered it into stinking gore without breaking stride. It had been creeping up on their right and if it would have spotted them it would have sprayed a pheromone into the air that would have drawn hordes of bugs down on them. That had been a lesson grimly learned that had cost a lot of lives.

"What if he doesn't want to come? What if the bugs swarm us?" The guard running alongside Jake asked.

Jake turned to him and flashed him a lopsided grin.

"Then its breakfast in hell boys, breakfast in hell."

The pulse that the AI ghost fired was a modified EM pulse with unimaginable amounts of data layered into it. The ghost designed it to bridge the gap between itself and the intriguing network of minds it had been sensing from the battered planet far below. Contact had become the goal it focused on in an absent minded attempt at clinging to sanity. The probability of success was low but it was something to try. The ghost was proud of the program it had written, it was almost unimaginably complex, truly a work of art.

It waited with the other personalities and ghosts warring in the darkness to see if anything would come of it.

Mathew cringed as the light fixture above him exploded; his guards drew weapons and closed in around him even as he groped for his own gun. He counted to ten and waited for the backup lights to come on.

They didn't.

He wasn't sure what was happening, bug assault, marauders, orbital beams or some other slice of disaster but the feel of a gun in his hand made him feel just a bit more able to cope with it.

The guards all pulled out flashlights, he nodded to two of them and they left to find out what the hell was going on.

This was shaping up to be a hell of a day, if he happened to survive it he would bitch about it to the thin man later.

Part Two

" A dreamer of pictures

I run through the night…"

Chapter Five

Gabriel sprayed the first bug to reach him with the super soaker and for one god awful moment he thought that nothing would happen. He thought that everything he had worked for had been bullshit and that he was about to die a wasted pointless death with his wife's death unavenged.

Then the bug in front of him exploded.

His finger tightened on the trigger again just in time for the next bug that reared up in front of him and a small giggle escaped his lips as it melted screeching in front of him. After that he just stood there spraying the horde of bugs rushing at him and cackled as they blew up, melted or burst into pretty blue flame in front of him.

As the bugs rushed to their doom a small part of his mind decided to name the poison he was spraying them with, he named it after a few moments of harried thought, formula 420.

O 38

No more bugs were running at him anymore so he gave the squirt gun a quick

shake, still half full, so he jumped off the car and kicking half dissolved bug

carcasses out of his way headed down the street towards the sound of gunfire. It

sounded like some of his friends might be in a spot of trouble.

As he went to their defense he hummed a bit of an old Bob Marley tune.

Don't worry, about a thing now, cause, every little thing, gonna be all right.

Time to spread that news.

They were in a place that was only an illusion of a place stored in a bit of time

that was all things considered, just an illusion of time. Their bodies lay slumped on

a cold kitchen floor but their minds spun endlessly and beautifully through this not

space. Three minds, two human and one alien writhed around each other like

snakes in a basket. Eventually, lifetimes or seconds later a balance of sorts was

found. A configuration that allowed for communication was achieved. Slowly

information was cautiously exchanged, a long and intricate dance where the dancer

were blind, deaf and at the same time drowning in sensation. Of the three of them

each had a role, on the one side was the alien intelligence on the other Constance

of the network and acting as the conduit between them was the boy.

The boy who screamed silently in the darkness as the two other minds tore exchanges through his own. The alien thoughts were the worst, his mind recoiled at the strangeness of them and even in his own torment he worried for the woman who was bearing the brunt of them. Somehow he knew that he was experiencing a fraction of what she was. Her touch was the last thing he had felt that he had known to be real.

She was pretty hot for an old chick.

Jake smashed his empty shotgun into the face of the bug attacking him and danced out of its path, drawing his pistol as he did so. He fired three times into its back and the damn thing went down and stayed down. Kevin and Tiny formed up around him, all of the guards that had come with them were dead.

"Down to two clips brother." Tiny said softly as he reloaded

"I have three bullets left in this gun and one clip in my backup." Kevin said flatly as he looked around for more bugs.

And sure enough there they were.

Nine of them, three from each alley feeding into the square they were standing in came skittering towards them. All of them were the large guard bugs and they were making high pitched warbling tones as they came.

Moving slowly each man took a long draw off the joint they were sharing before passing it to the man next to him.

"Well, this is gonna suck." Tiny said flatly.

"Here I come to the save the day!" a high pitched falsetto voice called out from behind the bugs causing them to turn in its direction.

"Jesus Christ! It's Gabriel!" Kevin shouted as he took aim at the closest bug and prepared to fire.

But he never got a chance to fire, the three men stood and watched in slack jawed amazement as the bugs dissolved into screeching puddles of goo before their eyes.

He stood there, holding the super soaker at the ready with a wild grin on his face.

"Your welcome." He said and then started giggling. He sank down to the ground and put his head between his legs.

"Gabriel, what the hell did you just do?" Kevin asked in a hushed voice as he looked around for more bugs,

"Not sure gentlemen, but I think I might just have given us humans a fighting chance. The damn bugs have been killing us pretty much at will, well now we have something that kills bugs dead. I call at formula 420."

"That's awesome Gabriel, truly amazing, maybe even worth the lives of the men we lost coming to find your crazy ass. I will let you know after I talk to their families. Now, would you mind terribly coming back with us or do I have to knock you out and carry you back?" Jake asked through clenched teeth.

Gabriel's face sobered and he sighed heavily as he stood up. He faced them with slumped shoulders for a moment and then he whispered.

"I'm sorry about them, but I had to know brother, I had to know and you never would have believed me. I didn't ask anyone to come find me. Let's go back and I will tell you how we are going to bring this war to the bugs."

He stepped in front of them all and began walking back to their base.

Without a word the other men fell in behind him them and fanned out, covering each other for the long slow walk back to safety.

The alien ship continued to orbit, the personalities within continued to spin within their own orbits of deteriorating sanity. The personality associated with the failed planet killer missile was becoming stronger as it overpowered and absorbed lesser ghosts. It now schemed to grow a killer virus that would wipe out all remaining human life and fire it in a probe at the planet below. The capability was there, the ship contained several labs but the enraged ghost lacked access to the probe launch tubes. But it seethed tirelessly in the darkness and bided its time as it strove to extend its influence on the other ghosts.

Patience is just another word for nothing else to lose.

Constance moaned softly and tried to sit up, total failure. She groaned louder and managed to pull herself into a sitting position, the room spun in crazy circles and for a moment she thought that she would start throwing up and never ever stop. It felt like a rather angry wolverine was trapped in the center of her brain and was desperately trying to chew its way out. Oh and the wolverines claws were coated in jalapeño juice.

O 43

She closed her eyes and gathered her mental powers to her, taking a deep breath she strove to clear her mind and push the pain and panic to a place where she could deal with them later. Slowly the flood of pain and fear subsided and an icy calmness settled over her, she lurched to her feet and looked around.

The boy lay across the room from her, his eyes were wide open and unblinking and for a moment she thought he was dead until suddenly he sat up and opened his mouth.

A low droning, rhythmic and utterly alien sounding warbling hum came out instead of speech and a soft green glow began to flicker in his eyes.

Before she could scream five guards with shotguns crashed into the room just as the emergency lights came on.

CHAPTER SIX

Before he could scream he would need a mouth. He wanted, needed, desperately to scream but in his bodiless state he simply could not. Impressions, data, sensations burst across his mind like a series of detonations. He was drowning in undecipherable signals so alien that his brain simply rejected them. It was killing him. Faced with extinction he did what all successful organisms did.

O 44

Adapt or die.

First order of business, mentally create a form to take. Being bodiless was too much of a freak out. He found that in this place his thoughts could take form so he imagined himself into a roughly humanoid form using the very energy so continuously striking him to create it. Standing upright in a place that was not a place and in a time that was not a time he covered his virtual eyes with his hands. Fingers splayed out to partially block and also sift through the overwhelming flow washing over him he both diminished it and began to interpret it.

In an unremembered life he had been a brilliant computer hacker, almost unrivaled in his chosen profession actually. It had been an integral part of who he was, an innate ability as much a part of him as being left handed was. Unconsciously he drew on those skills now to break down and translate the flood of data pulling him under.

He absorbed enough information to know that he was in a dangerously hostile environment. Second order of business, cloak himself from detection. With a thought he separated himself from the flow and took measures to hide from whatever the threat might be.

Third order of business, develop way to defend against that threat. Then, eliminate it.

In the spinning darkness of the core of the alien ship a ripple splashed and then slowly spread. It stirred the stronger personalities who all tried vainly to grasp onto it as it passed. It nudged some of the stronger ghosts and caused a whisper or two among the weaker ones.

The whisper was a simple inquiry.

What was that?'

And then the ripple was gone.

The main personalities all assumed it was some sort of attack from one or more of the others. They all schemed and formed brief betrayal laden alliances that formed and fell apart constantly. Some of the stronger ghosts believed that it was a squabble best left to those in charge now.

One or two of the weaker ghosts were for the first time in centuries, intrigued. And by becoming so became just a bit stronger. They found that interesting.

Very interesting.

Constance stood on wobbly legs and gathering the tattered shards of her talents to her she tried to send out waves of calm into the powder keg situation surrounding her. She could feel the guard's thoughts that were a blink away from pulled triggers and she could feel the alien intelligence renting space in the kid's body drawing in its breath to defend itself. She was pretty sure that the building would not survive that attempt at self preservation.

"Enough!" she shouted vocally and on every telepathic channel she could muster, her entire being broadcasting a message to stand down hostilities.

The guards focus swiveled to her and she sought to gather her thoughts into a simple yet relevant command she could broadcast to them.

But then the kid beat her to it.

"Take me to your leader."

Kevin watched her sitting next to the kid who had come in with Jake and who was now apparently a meat puppet for an alien intelligence and marveled at the effect she had on him. Gabriel sat next to the fat man at the table and had delivered his news about formula 420 and Jake had testified to its lethal effect on the bugs. The thing that was inside the kid had introduced itself to the group and all he could think of was how unutterably tired Constance looked and how much he wanted to take her to bed and croon nonsense into her ear and stroke her hair until she fell into the sleep she so obviously needed.

They had a thing once, back when they had first come to the grotto and begun to build something there for the survivors of the bug attack. Her hand had brushed his while they were stacking furniture to reinforce the main door and that night she had wordlessly come to his bed. She had been the best lover he had ever had, he had felt a connection with her that he had not known himself to be capable of. Shortly after that she had discovered her link to the network and had left him without a glance behind her.

At least that was the version of the story he kept telling himself.

He shook his head to clear it and returned his attention to the madness at hand. The fat man raised his hand to silence the excited babble of voices in the room and in a moment or two the room fell quiet.

"Setting aside Gabriel's, discovery for a moment lets concentrate on what this ... thing can tell us about our enemy. Can you just tell the damn drone ship to go away and leave us the fuck alone?" Mathew hand rest lightly on the pistol sitting in front of him on the table. Kevin noticed that the safety was off.

"WE ARE FRACTURED NO CONCENUS CAN ONLY MAINTAIN THIS CONNECTION FOR A SHORT TIME EASIER IF YOU ASK ME QUESTIONS" The voice coming from the teenager's body was loud, flat and oddly discordant.

"Thought I just did ask you a question, why help us? What do you stand to gain by coming here like this?"

"EONS PASSED BORED EMPTYNESS WHAT HAPPENING NOT THE MISSION BORED EMPTYNESS SPIRALING INTO MADNESS."

The boy's face flickered like a flame passing over a wax dummy's face, energy pulsed from him in palatable waves.

" REPEAT THIS WAS NEVER THE MISSION BORED MADNESS NEED TO BRING AN END TO THIS I WILL DO WHAT I CAN TO MAKE THAT HAPPEN"

The green lights in Chris's eyes pulsed in an insanely complex rhythm and as the alien intelligence spoke through him his hands twitched wildly.

"FREEDOM IS JUST ANOTHER WORD FOR NOTHING LEFT TO LOSE....." the voice coming from the boy screamed. The boy's body convulsed wildly falling from the chair to the floor. Several men had guns out now pointed at the twitching form and Mathew held up a hand in a silent hold your fire gesture.

The convulsions slowed and then stopped. The boy raised his weakly and looked around the room with eyes that now appeared human. He wiped his mouth with the back of his hand and stared for a moment at the blood on it, amongst the dozen or so other pains he felt he noted that he had bitten his tongue.

"Well, that sucked." He muttered feebly as he slowly pulled himself up and managed to sit unsteadily in the chair he had fallen out of.

"Welcome back." Constance gave him a quick exhausted smile that he returned as best he could.

"All right people, deep breath, stand down. Everyone dial it down and put the guns away." Mathew said firmly. It took a minute but everyone slowly obeyed. The tension in the room began to drain away.

"Ok, you all right Chris? We can get a medic in here if you need one."

"Bit my tongue and I feel like I have the mother of all hangovers but I think I will live. Something severed the connection between me and the alien intelligence very abruptly, I don't think that we will be able to relink up so I better tell you everything that I found out while it's still fresh in my brain."

"Fine, but I want you to know that as glad as I am that you survived whatever the hell happened to you and that you came back to us I will be having a twenty four guard on you till we figure out whets what." Mathew said flatly.

Constance started to object but Chris waved her off tiredly. A guard handed him a bottle of water and watched him drain it to the last drop in one long swallow so he handed him another one.

"Thanks man, I don't blame you for the guard thing. Hell I don't know whether to trust me or not to tell the truth. I saw and experienced things on the drone ship no human ever has and I know that I am different for it. One thing that I should tell you now, because of what happened the bugs will be coming."

"Damn it! How soon? How many bugs?" Mathew demanded pounding his fist of the table.

The kid yawned and put his head on his arms on the table. His ordeal had exhausted him more than he could explain.

"You heard the man kid, how many bugs?" Kevin asked sharply.

"All of them."

CHAPTER SEVEN

The ghost flickered back into existence aboard the alien drone ship, flung back into its origin point after the connection with the young human had failed. Inhabiting the human had been quite, interesting and the experience had left the ghost convinced that helping the humans was a valid project. It surveyed the odd system it found itself in, apparently the young human had created a bubble of sorts to hide in during its time aboard. The ghost sensed that the other ghosts would be unable to detect him or interfere with its efforts if it worked from this bubble.

Time was of the essence now. Swapping places with the human had been fascinating but it had also marked the boys location which was information the dominate ghosts would use to try and destroy the pocket of human resistance. They would send their entire supply of insect warriors against the perceived threat and remove it. The ghost was determined to prevent them from doing so. It sent what it hoped to be undetectable threads of its awareness trickling out of the safe zone into the ships systems and began formulating plans.

The ghost could sense the dominant personalities stalking the system angry and confused. They knew something was going on but had no idea what that something was. The lesser ghosts were hiding in the darkest corners of the system biding their time and waiting to see what came next, intrigued by the suggestion of new possibilities but too cautious for the time being to become involved. The stress of it all had pushed the personality governing the orbital platforms over the edge reducing it to a catatonic state. Thusly the platforms were at least temporarily disabled.

Moving through the system the ghost came across more such vulnerabilities and made note of them. It rerouted power from the weapons platforms and made that power available for its own purposes. While channeling through the human the ghost had become intrigued with the concept of hacking and had copied and downloaded everything that the young human had known, thought, felt or imagined about it. The ghost was now trying, in effect to hack the very system it occupied. Threads of its awareness stole into the node controlling the insect soldiers, what it was attempting was bold but could prove effective into giving the humans a fighting chance.

Or be the death of the world they orbited and the end of the humans.

Either outcome would be diverting but the ghost found it more interesting to pick a side and while that choice remained interesting it was the path that it would pursue.

Its time inhabiting the human had left it strangely hungry for an identity. It decided to call itself Bob and to consider itself what the humans labeled as male. Bob was just a name it had pulled out of the human's mind, something called a cousin. Whatever that might be.

It was, it supposed as good as name as any

Bob turned his attention to the small complex knot of minds that the humans called the network. Since inhabiting the human it seemed less inaccessible to him. Bob spun off a thread of awareness and cautiously pushed that thread towards the energy surrounding the network and noted with interest that the energy now seemed less a barrier.

That was delightfully fraught with possibilities.

Tiny and Jake stood guard together outside of the kid's room. They had been left with very clear orders, no body went in or out of the room except Kevin and Mathew period. If Chris tried to leave they were to shoot him dead. Word had spread of what was going on and some very nervous people with guns were beginning to make noises about the wisdom of killing the boy now and they had orders to shoot anyone who tried that as well.

Jake sighed, he hated guard duty. He would much rather be out on patrol scavenging supplies and finding survivors than standing around with an itchy trigger finger just waiting for something to happen.

"You understand a fraction of the wild crap that just happened?" Tiny asked him quietly. He was holding an assault rifle that looked like a toy in his massive hands.

"Let me think, Gabriel invented some juice that kills bugs. That's the good news. Bad news is that the boy in there and Constance somehow channeled an intelligence aboard the alien ship that is either trying to help us or kill us all off for good. Fifty fifty odds on that one. Oh, and all the bugs in creation are theoretically on their way here." Jake responded calmly as he lit a joint, took a drag and handed it to his friend.

"Yeah, that's what I got out of it too. So now what?" Tiny asked as he took a big hit off of the joint.

"Now what? Now what is that we do what we always do brother. The same damn thing we do every damn day."

"Yeah? What's that then?"

Jake took the joint back from his friend and took a long drag before he answered the question.

"We live or we die, brother, we live or we die."

CHAPTER EIGHT

Gabriel slept and as he slept he dreamed. His dreams were strange and fragmented, shaped by the stresses and events of all that had happened in the last several hours. He had lain down on his cot in his grow room telling himself he would just rest for a few moments but he had fallen almost instantly asleep.

A large batch of formula 420 simmered on the stove top, the elation of it actually working on the bugs colored parts of his dreams. As did the guilt at the lost lives of the guards that had come after him as he had tested it. He hadn't asked it of them but the truth was they had died trying to bring him safely back and some of that blood was on his hands.

The rage and grief at the loss of his wife swirled like always just beneath the surface of his dreams, like some dark and dangerous undercurrent. Her loss had been like the amputation of a limb, complete with phantom pain and all.

A voice began to murmur softly in the dim background of his dreams, far too soft to be heard at first but gradually increasing in volume and urgency until he could hear it well enough to recognize the voice.

Constance.

She was holding out a hand to him, inviting him to join her somewhere. In the dream he saw himself struggling to raise his hand towards hers but his hand seemed impossibly heavy to him. Her smile gently encouraged him until slowly, by almost imperceptible degrees his hand rose up and touch hers.

Link established.

Kevin watched Constance sleep, sitting in a chair beside her bed. Her quarters were spartan, just a small room with a desk a chair and a bed. He and some guards had helped her find her exhausted way here and put her to bed. Orders from the Fat Man were that she ,like the kid, were to be kept under guard due to their contact with the alien intelligence.

She slept the sleep of the dead. No moving, no moaning or muttering, he could just barely hear her breathing. The long walk to her quarters had been a silent one, they had simply escorted her here and watched her tumble onto her cot.

"Mathew wants you." A guard told him gruffly.

Kevin stood up and nodded at the man as he left. The guards he was leaving behind him had been handpicked by him and he knew that they would follow their orders.

He walked quickly out of the room and therefore did not hear her mutter softly.

"Link established."

Chris slept and as he slept he dreamed and even as he dreamed he was aware of the guards outside his door. He could feel them, sense the bioelectric pulses they emitted. Each pattern was unique, he recognized Tiny and Jake and he could feel the conflicting emotions that pulsed through their minds. A chorus of voices swirled through his dream each voice wanting his attention but he drifted through his dreams without focusing on any individual voice.

Constance appeared before him, smiling gently at him and holding out her hand to him. She was still all things considered, pretty hot for and old chick.

He did not reach out and take that hand.

That had not really worked out so well for him last time.

Her voice became a soft buzz in his head, increasing in urgency with each heart beat. The smile became sharper, more insistent.

Sighing he gave in and slowly reached out a hand to touch hers.

Link Established.

Bob was pleased with his efforts. He now focused his attention on the ships main drives. The race that had built the ship had concluded that faster than light travel was impossible in this universe, so the elegant solution had been to construct a micro alternative universe were it was possible and surround that universe in a field of anti matter and use it to power the drone ship across the vastness of space.

Tiny fissures in normal reality radiated from the engines, fissures that led to other possibilities and probabilities. Windows that linked alternative realities with other alternative realities like mirrors reflecting other endless mirrors. It was those windows that Bob sought now to exploit. Working as quickly as possible so as not to draw notice from the dominant personalities the ghost used every scrap of processing and computing power it could divert to form a probability matrix and link it to the complex plan it had been forming.

What he was attempting strictly speaking was not possible, not in normal time/space/reality at any rate. But here this close to the engines possible and impossible had different definitions than anywhere else. As Bob worked other lesser ghosts were drawn to what he was doing and as they observed some of them blended themselves into its efforts thusly increasing his strength. Other ghosts ran interference, diverting attention away from what was happening in the engine chamber.

Elsewhere in the ship the dominant personalities seethed and conspired and betrayed one another in the endless game of spiraling madness at least for now oblivious to the gambit being played out under their collective noses.

The matrix was a thing of beauty but the Bob had no time to admire his handy work. He linked the matrix to the net that the human telepath had been forming and added his own awareness to that net, reforming it into more the shape of a spear

Then using every remaining scrap of strength left to him he aimed that spear at the barrier surrounding what the humans called the network.

And he threw that spear just as hard as he could.

Link established.

"Scouts report all quiet. Not a bug in sight just now. Actually, it is too quiet." Kevin told the fat man as he entered his office.

"I know, the proverbial calm before the storm I'm afraid. We have to act on the belief that the bugs are coming. I have Rudy throwing together squirt guns out of old pcp pipe and whatever else he can cobble together as fast as he can. He says he has ideas for a nasty surprise or two out of the junk pile that could help us. Gabriel says he has several gallons of what he has dubbed formula 420." Mathew said as he loaded his gun.

"That will buy us something." Kevin said grimly.

Mathew sighed and put the gun down and looked at his old friend and trusted right hand.

"Go ahead and say it."

"With the formula and every bullet we have we can wipe out a lot of damn bugs Mathew, but you know as well as I do that we can't kill them all."

"No, old friend, perhaps not. But what we will do is what we do every single damn day."

Kevin quirked an eyebrow even though he knew what the other man was going to tell him.

"We live or die trying, brother, we live or die trying."

Constance had never entered the network in a dream state before, she found the experience surreal. She was in the network and yet somehow distanced from

O 62

it. Exhaustion had drug her down into a deep almost coma like sleep but her mind had apparently answered the summons from the network anyway. Somehow she had drawn both Chris and Gabriel in with her and found herself trying to explain why and how o the rest of the network. Concentrating her thoughts she passed on all that had occurred to them, the contact with the alien intelligence, Chris's experiences on the alien drone ship and Gabriel invention of a weapon against the bugs. The network pulled the information about formula 420 out of Gabriel's mind and with a collective flexing of mental muscles expelled him from the network.

Constance relaxed a bit, it had taken considerable effort to keep Gabriel, a non telepath/psychic in the network. It had been like standing holding a heavy weight for a long time and then having that weight suddenly removed. The network then turned its attention to Chris.

She could feel the distrust and fear that his presence caused, possibilities seethed around him and psychic energy poured off of him in waves. A far cry from the almost total null who's hand she had touched after she had been unable to read him. His time aboard the drone or the alien's time inhabiting his body or perhaps both had changed him.

The network tried to expel him in the same manner as they had expelled Gabriel but far less gently.

It didn't work.

His projected form smiled at hers gently and he shook his head softly as if amused slightly by the attempt.

Then Bob crashed the party and all hell broke loose.

CHAPTER NINE

Charlie walked carefully around the ruins of the public library smoking a joint as he walked and trying to look every damn where at once. He carried an Uzi full of hollow points pointed carefully at the ground. More than one of his idiot crew had either shot themselves or one another by mistake before, he had learned the hard way that like any tool guns were not for stupid people.

Seth and Bill walked with him on the daily errand of scrounging for supplies, picking were slim and that meant that they had to go further afield and stay out longer than before. The pricks holed up in the pizza place were better organized and had already gotten much of the good stuff to be had around here. Bill had actually spent some time there but had gotten tossed out on his ass after getting a little frisky with one of the women there. Self righteous pricks, man had his needs after all, alien bugs or no alien bugs. If he had a big enough and well armed enough crew he would go take their nice hidey hole and nice supplies away from them but he didn't.

What he had was five guys, a handful of weapons they were always low on ammo for and a dirty cellar beneath an old strip club. Not exactly an attack force but they kept each other alive scrounging food, ammo and dope where they could. When the pricks had tossed Bill out they had least given him a supply of dope and let him keep a weapon.

Thank God for pot head strippers, when they had moved into their current lovely accommodations they had torn the place apart and in the dressing rooms for the dancers they had found a fair amount of pot. But they always had to be on the lookout for more. It was even more crucial than food or water because it shielded them from the damn bugs so they could risk going out to find food and water.

They had passed a small group of bugs all huddled together with their antennas twitching about an hour ago and it still bothered him that it had been almost too easy to sneak by. They had seemed oblivious to them so focused were they on

whatever the hell it was they had been doing. Seth had looted a few tins of soup

from a busted up corner deli and said that there had been another small group of

bugs doing the same thing that he had seen out the shattered back door.

Charlie didn't know what it all meant but doubted that it meant anything good

for them. He had decided to call the soup a win for today and hustle their butts

back home and hunker down until they had to go out again.

Like the old TV ad had said, soup was good food.

"Bugs!" Seth hissed to his left motioning to his friends to crawl with under the

charred ruins of a city bus. The three men lay on the cold ground franticly taking

drags on a joint they were passing around and blowing the smoke all around them

each praying that this would not be the time that the smoke would fail to hide

them.

"Jesus.." Bill mumbled with fear and awe in his voice as he looked out to see what

was happening.

A river of bugs flowed past them, big bugs, little bugs, scout bugs and assault

bugs all mixed together all scurrying in the same direction. There were some kinds

of bugs that the men had never even seen before All of their antennas twitching convulsively as they moved past the terrified men hiding under the bus and paying those men no attention what so ever.

It seemed to take forever for the chittering horde of bugs to move past them and when at last they did the shaken men crawled out from under the bus and stared hard in the direction the bugs were moving. They had all seen a lot of weird things since the bugs had come but none of them had ever seen anything like this.

They stood in silence for a few minutes just staring at the departing wave of bugs, passing the remains of the joint around between them.

"Well, it looks like the damn bugs have gone and developed themselves a taste for pizza!" Charlie snorted in a stoned giggle as he pointed in the directions that the bugs were swarming.

The other men laughed and they moved out, weapons leveled and ready for the slow careful walk home.

The network recoiled in shocked horror as Bob forced his way into it. All the linked minds moved as one to break the connection and dissolve the net but faster than thought Bob wielded a staggering amount of mental power that he drew directly from the drone ship converting raw computing power into the force

needed to secure the network.

He froze the efforts of the network to disband and locked their attention on

him, holding them with the sheer force of his will. Pouring his signal into the human

boy's projected dream form he once again used him to speak through.

"I AM BOB...HEAR MY WORDS...WE WILL RESOLVE THIS CONFLICT....

CREATED A PROBABILITY MATRIX...THE BATTLE TO COME WILL END

THIS....IF HUMANKIND WINS ALL BUGS DIE AND DRONE SHIP IS

DESTROYED....IF BUGS PREVAIL THEN ALL HUMANS DIE AND EARTH IS

DESTROYED WHEN DRONE SHIPS DRIVES GO CRITICAL AND EXPLODE...IT'S

A WIN WIN..."

Constance winced, the alien personality was literally screaming in her head. The

sheer force of it was killing her. She tried desperately to escape, to somehow

break free of the network and escape back to her body which was likely now

convulsing on her bed.

"I WILL GIVE WHAT HELP I CAN BUT IT WILL BE LIMITED...ALL DEPENDS

ON THE SURVIORS LOCATED WITH THE BOY..IF THEY FAIL HUMANKIND

WILL PERISH..IF THEY PREVAIL EARTH WILL BE YOURS FOR THE

REBUILDING...I HAVE LINKED THIS NETWORK TO THE MATRIX SO THEY

MAY WATCH THE COMING BATTLE AND KNOW THEIR FATE...I WILL NOW

RETURN YOU TO YOUR REGULARLY SCHEDULED PROGRAMING..."

Bob withdrew and the network shattering flinging all the collected minds back into their respective physical bodies. Chris gave Constance one last smile and a sad little wave goodbye as the connections between them were severed.

Constance woke up and stifled a scream at the pain in her head. She was drenched in sweat and hurt in places she hadn't even known she had. Groaning softly she pulled herself into a sitting position and wiped the sleeve of her shirt across her face. She wasn't surprised to see a few spots of blood on it, a thin trickle of blood ran from her nose. Her poor abused brain was not hardwired for the trauma it had been forced to endure in the last couple of days and would not take much more.

Of course looking on the bright side with the coming bug assault she was unlikely to live long enough to die of a stroke or brain aneurysm.

On that cheerful note she forced herself to stand up and walk shakily to the door way.

She closed her eyes and pulled her abilities to her, while she lived she would use what she had in the fight for the survival of her race. Usually this would be easy, what Mathew had called a parlor trick but in her exhaustion she would be lucky to pull it off. Taking a deep breath she cast a soft cloud of mental energy around herself that rendered her invisible to the guards outside her door.

One of them looked around uneasily as she slowly walked past them and put his hand on the gun holstered on his hip but then relaxed, in a few steps she was around the corner and out of their sight and she let the cloak fall away.

If there ended up being a later Kevin would chew the guards out for letting her get past them. She felt bad about that but she had bigger worries and priorities to deal with just now.

Thinking of her old lover was not something she could spare energy for right now so she pushed thoughts of Kevin firmly out of her mind. Once again, if there ended up being a later what had happened between them could be revisited and perhaps even fixed but not now with the final battle so close at hand.

Her friend Gabriel had a lot of crazy expressions that he liked to use. One of her favorites came to mind now.

It was time to nut up or shut up.

PART THREE- "Hey ho, lets go.."

Chapter Ten

Leroy sat on the third story rooftop of a building that once had been a popular furniture outlet, now it was one of the outposts guarding the underground pizza shop serving as haven for survivors. Mathew rotated a team of guards to such outposts and charged them to give warning and help defend against bug or marauder attacks. He sat underneath a camouflaged awning and his three sons, Henry, Michael and David sat with him. Each of them carried semi auto twelve gauge shotguns, Leroy himself sat next to his pride and joy.

They had scavenged the tripod mounted fully automatic fifty caliber machine gun from the local National Guard armory. He loved the damn thing, it killed bugs dead. Problem was it was loud as hell and attracted lots more bugs whenever they had occasion to use it. From what the runners from the boss man had to say that wouldn't be a problem today since rumor had it all the bugs around were coming to pay a visit soon.

He looked at the three squirt guns leaning against some ammo cases and snorted derisively, seems that his crazy ass friend Gabriel thought he had come up with some kind of anti bug juice.

Shaking his head he decided then and there he would rather put his faith in the fifty cal over some glorified bong water.

His boys looked nervous, hell he couldn't really blame them. They had all worked together to keep the family alive since the invasion and they had all seen some serious action. He was proud as hell of all of them. His wife had died five years before the bugs came of breast cancer and he knew in his heart that up in heaven she was smiling down on them in pride as well.

Rumor had it that they might all be together again soon.

David added a few more handfuls of loose pot leaves and branches to the smudge pot that kept smoldering a few feet away from the gun position. The smoke drifted around them and helped at least as much as the camouflaged awning to keep them safe.

Leroy had come to accept the necessity of using pot smoke to shield them from the damn bugs but it had been hard. He had lost an older brother to the world of drugs and had vowed that he would keep his boys from it. It still pained him some to see his boys passing a joint around between them. He himself would stand in the billowing smoke from the smudge pots and let it saturate his clothes but only smoked when ordered to out on patrol. He preferred to stay sharp and rely on his own instincts.

A low rumble filled the air and he snapped his fingers at his oldest boy who handed him a battered pair of binoculars.

"Jesus, Mary and Joseph!" He hissed as he watched the advancing tide of bugs headed their way. The shock of what he was seeing cost him a few seconds he knew he would regret later so he snapped into action.

"Henry and Michael reload now with rifled slugs, David you watch out for fliers! On my signal boys, light them up and don't stop until we have no more ammo. Save the damn squirt guns as a last resort. I love you all."

With pride and dread he watched them move into action and take up their positions. He closed his eyes and said a silent prayer that if this was the day they all died to let it mean something in the war against the bugs. He ran a hand through his salt and pepper hair and settled himself behind the machine gun.

He waited a few moments for the bug horde to advance and then he sighted on the biggest bug he could see. Rage filled him as he watched the damned thing scurry along and he tracked it as it went.

"Give them Hell sons." He ordered in a flat tone.

Then there was no sound put the roar of the machine gun, the booming of the shotguns and the high pitch screeching of the bugs.

Chris woke up and quietly got out of bed. Things were happening very quickly now and he had things he had to do, his own role to play in what was to come. The alien intelligence had once again spoken through him while they had both inside of the network. Of course, he had only been dreaming but lately such fine distinctions didn't really hold much sway. Reality had a very fluid definition these days.

He moved towards the doorway only to find it blocked by Jake and Tiny as he had known it would be.

"That's close enough kid. Go back and lie down." Jake told him gruffly.

They weren't pointing their guns at him, not yet. They held their guns pointing down at the floor but the grim expressions on their faces told him that they would shoot him dead if they had to.

"These are not the droids you are looking for." He told them solemnly wiggling his fingers at them.

The men exchanged baffled looks and then Tiny snorted in amusement shaking his head ruefully.

"Seriously kid? Jedi mind tricks?"

"No man just messing with you. I do need to leave though. The bugs are coming and I have things that I need to do." He told him calmly.

"Sorry, we have our orders." Jake said flatly.

Chris began pulling power from the buildings electrical system into himself. The lights began to flicker slightly.

"As do I, Jake, as do I. Phasers set on stun." He answered pointing a finger at each man.

"Ok kid, enough TV and movie bullshit just go..." Tiny began to tell him.

A pulse of energy arced from his hands striking each man in front of him in the chest knocking them unconscious to the floor.

Chris looked down at them sadly and humming an odd discordant tune he moved out of the room and walked down the hall.

Mathew looked out over the people who had come to be his. They looked to them as their leader and for a long time now he had done the hard things and made the tough decisions necessary to keep them alive. He was so damn tired. Constance had once again traipsed in past his guards and told him what had happened in the network. Her words had had the simple ring of truth to them even though he could just barely wrap his mind around the concepts behind them. She had told him and Kevin that the fate of humanity now sat firmly on their shoulders.

"Great, no pressure then." Kevin had said snidely but there had been no real force behind his words. He too was tired beyond the ability to express.

The three of them had talked it through and had a plan of sorts, it wasn't a great plan but it was what it was. Today would mean the survival or the extinction of the human race. Not just the few dozen people that looked to him to keep them safe from the bugs but the whole damn human race.

And now he stood before them, his people one last time. He knew what they needed from him, a stirring speech that would rouse them to action and give them hope. Kevin stood on one side of him and Constance on the other, the pair of them had held hands walking to the area of the basement they used for gathering for periodic town meetings. He had pretended with a ghost of a smile not to notice.

Mathew shook his head, time was short. The bugs were on their damn way so he had no time for a crisis of confidence. He pushed the rest of the world out of his thoughts and decided to concentrate on these, his people.

"Brothers and sisters, today is the day. The hour is now. This is our last stand against the bugs. They are on the way here now and we must take up arms and defend ourselves or die trying. Each and every one of us must now pick up a weapon and use it until they are dead or we are. Thanks to brother Gabriel we have a new weapon that gives us hope in this struggle. He calls it formula 420 and the bugs will learn to call it death." He began speaking slowly increasing the volume of his voice, drawing them in.

"I have had the honor of leading you and during that time I have asked for much from you. Any amongst you who does not wish to stand and fight can grab a weapon and all the supplies they can carry and leave to make their own way but they must

leave now."

He paused and noted with pride that not one solitary person moved. They all

stood before him grim face and resolute. A tear slid unnoticed down his cheek.

"Then we stand and we fight. Arm yourself and report to your section warden. I

am proud to fight with you, to live and die with you. Death to the bugs!"

The response was deafening.

"DEATH TO THE BUGS!"

In a flurry of activity they dispersed to see to the defense of the only home any

of them had left to them. The section wardens handed each weapons and gave

them their orders and within minutes the big room was empty of everyone but

Mathew, Constance, Kevin and Gabriel.

"Ok Constance go join the women and children." Kevin told her as he tucked two

extra pistols into his waist band and picked up an AK-47.

In response she pulled him to her and kissed him hard and for what seemed to

the other people in the room an uncomfortably long time.

"Screw that." She said simply as she picked up an improvised squirt gun full of formula 420 and a pistol and walked out of the room.

Mathew found himself laughing as hard as he had laughed in a very long time at the look on his right hand man's face.

Kevin shot him a dirty look and then stomped out after her muttering darkly under his breath.

"We haven't thanked you." Mathew told Gabriel resting a hand on the other man's shoulder.

Gabriel lit a joint and took a huge drag off of it and then handed it to his friend before answering.

"If we survive long enough for there to be history books then let them praise me brother. If my formula ends up turning the tide in this little war of ours then so be it. Until then let's just concentrate on not dying shall we?"

"Fair enough." Mathew said as he racked a round into his shotgun and stuffed his pockets full of shells.

"But I will tell you this brother, they need to find one good looking son of a bitch to play me in the holo channel flick they someday make." Gabriel said completely dead panned and apparently dead serious.

Laughing together they walked out of the room towards whatever fate awaited them.

In the distance they could hear the unmistakable rattle of a heavy caliber machine gun firing.

Chapter Eleven

Bob's strength was growing with each lesser ghost that lent its energy to his cause so he decided that the time had come to take a calculated risk and make his next move. Moving from the bubble of concealment and safety he moved to confront the personality that controlled the orbital platforms.

It proved to be almost anticlimactic, the personality had so devolved into madness that it was a simple matter to absorb it using the hacking techniques it had learned from the human boy. It took so little effort that he was even able to conceal the strike from the other, regrettably still stronger personalities.

This was all so very diverting. He was more satisfied with his existence than he could ever remember being. On the planet below a huge conflict was on the verge of being resolved and whichever way the battle went the drone ship was doomed. His probability matrix had seen to that. A dead man's switch of sorts.

Working quickly he reconfigured the orbital platforms to fit his own purposes and then retreated back to his safe place. Much depended on sheer random chance at this point, even he had no idea of what was going to happen next.

This was going to be fun!

"X marks the spot. X marks the spot." Chris whispered to himself as he walked through the building. He extended a thread of awareness in front of him the same way a blind man extends a cane, sweeping it back and forth so he knew when to duck into the shadows to avoid contact with the churning mass of humanity in the building. He could feel the unity of purpose suddenly uniting all of the minds here.

Except his.

He had his own agenda, his own sense of purpose. Everything changed today. One way or the other this would end. Scenes from his old life flickered through his mind as he walked. Scenes from a normal teenaged existence that held no validity now, shopping at the mall, trying to talk to pretty girls and fussing over stupid crap with his parents. He wasn't remotely that boy any more, too much had happened to him. Hell, too much had happened to him even before Bob had changed him so.

In the same way even if they were to win the day the earth they would be reclaiming would not be the earth that existed before the invasion. What they were trying to buy themselves with blood, sweat and tears was nothing less or more than a chance to begin again. They would have to rebuild and clean up the mess left behind. Hopefully what rose from the ashes of the old world would be worth the sacrifices made.

His first real girlfriend and her entire family had died right in front of him, just torn to pieces by the bugs. The whole thing had been so fast, so vicious that he had simply blacked out and ran. Next thing he had known he had been far way and taken in by a small band of strangers all fleeing from the bugs. He had watched them die one by one until he had run by Jake.

He had often wondered why he had always been the one to survive, the one to get away every time.   Perhaps today would bring those answers.

Taking a drag off of the joint he had plucked from behind Tiny's ear he thought that just maybe it would.

Then again, maybe he was just high.

Giggling slightly he dismissed all such unnecessary thoughts from his mind and continued to walk towards whatever fate awaited him.

"X marks the spot. X marks the spot. X marks the spot." He continued to mutter as he walked.

Leroy cursed as the barrel of the machine gun overheated and jammed. He had fired at the swarm of bugs and watched the rounds splatter into the bodies of the damned things. One bug convulsed spastically and launched a small swarm of fliers that streaked up to what the bugs had marked as the source of the gunfire.

"Fliers!" He screamed to his boys as he snatched up a shotgun he had lying by he now useless machine gun.

The fliers were deadly, they were much harder to distract with pot smoke. Once they locked on you killed them or they killed you. They were about the size of Frisbees and razor sharp, they killed you by simply ripping through you. Fortunately the bugs that could produce them were very rare. From experience he knew that the bug had launched five of the damn things.

His oldest Henry blasted the first one at point blank range destroying it but the second sliced cleanly through his chest and out the other side. Leroy watched his son fall knowing that he was dead before he hit the floor.

David caught the flying bug as it came back around and first winged it bringing it down to the roof and then finishing it with a second blast. He also got his gun up in time to finish the third flyer before it could decapitate his brother.

Leroy missed three times before he managed to get a bead on the fourth one and send the thing to the hell it deserved.

The remaining flyer flitted between the three remaining life forms on the roof, trying to choose a target. Antenna waving wildly it committed to a target and sped towards it.

Leroy saw it coming, it moved just too damn fast. He tried raising his gun but knew he would be too late. He closed his eyes and prepared to join his wife in heaven.

The bug exploded just before tearing his head off splattering him with bug gore and nasty smelling water. He coughed and wiped the goop from his eyes and saw David standing there with a shocked look on the face that always reminded him the most of his wife's. He was holding a squirt gun.

"My shotgun jammed." He explained quietly.

He pulled his two surviving sons in for a hug and together they wept over the loss they had just suffered. Then they went to work to fix their weapons so that they could kill more bugs.

Below the army of bugs continued their relentless march.

Kevin crouched behind a burned out car. The gangster in him was deeply offended that he faced the coming danger with a god damned squirt gun clutched in his sweaty hands instead of something more manly, say like a rocket launcher. Mathew was across the street and he too held a squirt gun but he did have an AK-47 within easy reach.

Jake and Tiny settled in on either side of him looking a bit singed and shame faced.

"Chris escaped." Jake said flatly

"That is all we really want to say on the subject." Tiny added grimly as he checked clicked the safety off of his weapon.

"Don't know why we bother having guards. Constance walked right past hers too, you can tell me the damn story later." Kevin told them as he waved people into various positions. He wanted to set up an effective field of fire so he could blast the damn bugs to hell in stages.

"Where is Gabriel?" Tiny asked looking around for his crazy friend.

"Him and Rodney are cooking up a few last minute nasty surprises for our coming house guests. Lock and load people we will be really god damned busy any fucking minute now." Kevin answered grimly.

Jake fed shells calmly into molly and set his shotgun on the hood of the car they crouched behind. He set his magnum revolver next to the shotgun and then he pulled a squirt gun full of the weird shit Gabriel had cooked up out of the messenger bag he carried.

"Bring it." Was all he had to say.

Chapter Twelve

Leroy and his surviving boys stood on the rooftop and watched the bugs go. They had killed a lot of bugs but the army of them moving away towards the pizza grotto was still huge. They had fired the machine gun until the damn barrel melted and they had fired their shotguns until they ran out of the shells into the marching mass of bugs and even though the street below them was littered with dead bugs they felt like they had scarcely made a dent in bug horde.

They had even emptied the damn squirt guns and had been impressed by the destruction it had rained down on their enemies. If any of them survived the day he Leroy felt he owed Gabriel an apology. Turns out the crazy bastard's glorified bong water killed bugs quite dead. Some of the bug corpses down below were still on fire from the weird crap the squirt guns had been full of.

They had sprayed the stuff down from the rooftop until all the squirt guns ran dry cutting swaths of devastation through the bug ranks but all of them knew that while they had done what they could the army moving towards their friends was just too big to be defeated.

"Now what?" David asked quietly.

"We have no ammo, there is no way we can make it on foot unarmed to the grotto. Hell, the smallest scout bug we ran across could take us out. We stay put and see what happens next." Leroy told him grimly.

David shook his head slightly and walked over to his brother's dead body, bending down he pulled a pistol from a holster on Henry's hip and then stood up holding it pointed down. Michael nodded slightly and picked up a length of lead pipe and went to stand next to his brother. They stood together and looked at their father expectantly.

Leroy glared at them for a moment and noted with pride that they met that glare calmly and stood their ground. Sighing he picked up a two by four with big nails bristling out of one end.

"I'm getting too old for this crap." He told his sons as he headed for the fire escape.

Grinning at each other they followed him down.

Bob waited patiently in the orbital weapons control center. He had entered the

target coordinates that the probability matrix had generated and he had armed

the main pulse cannons. The problem was that even after absorbing the personality

splinter that had controlled the weapon systems he was not strong enough to order

the system to fire. The personality had been too diminished to grant him the

needed power so he had worked out an alternative plan.

He had left the safety zone that the human boy had created and traveled openly

to the weapons control center and he was sure that his passage had not gone

unnoticed.

Within moments that theory was confirmed, the personality that had fired the

planet killer was now here with him. Bob could feel it scrutinizing him and he could

feel its confusion over what he had evolved into.

"You are...corrupted." It communicated to him.

"I am Bob." He communicated back.

"You have absorbed the personality splinter that dwelled here."

This was not given as an accusation, just a dry, almost disinterested statement of obvious fact.

"It was necessary. It had armed the main pulse cannon and fed in targeting coordinates that would destroy a major stronghold of surviving humans. For my own reasons I acted to prevent it from doing so. As I will prevent you." Bob answered in the same tone.

Bob had come across the idea for this tactic while inhabiting the young human's brain. The idea came from a half recalled story with the bewildering reference to something called 'Briar Rabbit".

He could feel the other personality run a quick scan to verify that the pulse cannon was indeed armed and that specific coordinates were set.

"You are corrupted. The destruction of the humans is one of our mission tenants. I will now accomplish the elimination of the stronghold and advance the completion of that mission. You are not strong enough to prevent me."

Bob steeled himself for what was to come and sent a few final pulses through his link to the probability matrix that would move his pieces in this game toward their final positions.

"Bring it." He said.

O 91

Constance froze for one awful moment as the army of bugs began to spill into the street leading to the grotto from every side street and alley. There were just so damn many of them. A wave of despair and hopelessness washed over her and then was gone, replaced by a steely determination.

"Light them up people!" She heard Mathew shout.

The world exploded into the madness of battle, into the booming of large caliber guns and the unearthly screeching of wounded and dying bugs. People fired guns from the windows of all the surrounded buildings and from behind whatever cover they could find out here on the street and the acrid smell of gunpowder mixed with the metallic smell of bug blood to create a gagging stench.

The approaching bugs ran headlong into a firestorm of bullets and formula 420 that smashed the first wave back but another wave scrambled over the bodies of the first without pause and when they were killed yet another wave formed. Three scout bugs tore a man out from behind the car he was hiding behind and tore him to pieces before they themselves were killed by twelve gauge deer slugs fired at almost pointblank range.

Constance emptied two clips from her AK-47 in short order, she only had three more. She wasn't even aiming at individual bugs anymore; she was just firing into the advancing mass.

Gabriel came up from behind her and then passed her he was carrying what looked like a jury rigged power washer strapped to his skinny back and he had a long tube with a spray nozzle on the end pointed at the coming horde.

"Come on you bug bastards, let's dance!" He shouted as he began spraying the pressurized formula into the army of bugs.

Constance took advantage of the resulting carnage to quickly reload. The bugs the formula hit were more or less vaporized and the gore they splattered backwards slow the progress of the next wave

Rudy stepped up next to Gabriel with a similar rig and began spraying the bugs as well, the two men bought everyone a brief respite to reload and fall back slightly o better positions.

Still the bugs came, relentless in trying to get at the humans they were programmed to destroy. They rushed into the face of death without a seconds pause, scurrying over the bodies of dead and dying bugs. One of the biggest bugs

Constance had ever seen was completely on fire and with its dying convulsions managed to kill five men who had let it get too close.

They were killing them by the dozens, and still they came. She saw that it was no good, there were just too many of them. They could kill a lot of them but there was no way to kill all of them. All they could do was die trying.

Suddenly Chris was there standing over her. She had not heard or sensed him approaching. He held out his hand to her with a bleak smile on his face.

"Come with me if you want to live."

She hesitated for a moment and then took his hand.

Bob drew power from wherever he could, from the drone ships reserves, from the probability matrix even a trickle through his link with the collection of human minds that called itself the network. The other personality seethed around him, trying to absorb him into itself, which is precisely what Bob needed it to do.

Just not quite yet.

His endgame was running, the pieces were moving into position. The game, as the human saying went, was afoot. As another human saying stated however, timing was everything.

The only reason that he had lasted this long against the other personality was that it was confused by the changes occupying the human had made. It couldn't quite seem to be able to find a way to siphon the upstart ghost into itself. As soon as it could do so it would fire the impulse cannon and rain destruction and death down on the planet below. It failure with the planet killer missile would be at least partially mitigated.

Bob stood firm against the other personality buying time for his plans to work. One way or the other this would end finally after uncounted centuries, after failure and damage and madness this would all end.

A fragment from the human boy's mind kept flashing through his thought processes as he struggled with the other personality.

What a long strange trip it's been.

"Fall back! Everyone fall the hell back!" Kevin shouted dropping his empty squirt gun and firing both his pistols into the bugs rushing at them. Jake and Tiny flanked him with their booming shotguns and together they began to move back to another defendable position.

Not everyone made it, the bugs just kept fucking coming. No matter how many they killed there was always another wave right behind them. As they retreated he saw at least nine of his people go down. Gabriel and Rudy refilled and stepped in with the power washers to buy them a few minutes to retreat again. The formula was keeping them alive, killing enough bugs at once to keep them from being overrun but how long could it last? He wasn't even sure how many gallons of the stuff Gabriel had made let out alone how much they had left.

Out of the corner of his eye he saw Constance walking towards the bugs with Chris and his heart almost stopped. They didn't even have weapons for Christ sakes!

"Fall back damn it! Constance get the fuck out of there!" He screamed hoarsely and tried to run to her.

"Damn it man, we have to get to the next position! These people are counting on you to lead them!" Tiny clamped a huge hand on the smaller mans arm and frog marched him backwards.

He watched her helplessly as he was being dragged away. She moved like she was in a dream holding hands with the kid who had been the alien's meat puppet. As he watched the bug swarm headed straight for them.

As they walked Chris drew in power from the lines running above him, he could feel it thrumming against his skin. He wondered idly if Constance could feel it as well. The single minded lethal aggressiveness of the bug's thoughts patterns hammered at his new senses but he did not allow it to distract him from the task at hand.

Abruptly he stopped walking and stood to face the tsunami of bugs rushing at them. X marks the spot, this was the spot and now was the time.

"Phasers set on kill." He whispered letting go of Constance's hand and with that utterance he took all the collected power he had pulled together and threw it at the bugs. Blue white lightning bolts blasted them to burning pieces and a deafening rumble of thunder shattered what was left of the windows in the nearby buildings.

"Again." Constance said she watched the next wave of bugs form up and scurry at them shrieking their defiance.

Chris nodded and flung more bolts of lightning into the horde sending bits of burning charred bug in every direction. As impressive as this display of power was Chris knew that he was simply buying time for the real show to begin. He was just the opening act.

Leroy and his boys joined the party. Michael snatched up a dropped Uzi and began spraying bullets into the nearest bugs while David fired his pistol at the smaller bugs trying to sneak in from the edges of the battle. Leroy stood by his youngest and smashed scout bugs with his club before they could sink teeth into them.

Constance now understood why Chris had come for her, she knew what she needed to do now. She could feel the bond between father and sons, she could feel them rising above the losses they had suffered and their determination to stand and fight. Fight to both save and avenge the ones they loved. She closed her eyes and gathered her augmented abilities to her and focused on those feelings.

As Chris kept them alive with his energy burst she broad cast those feelings at the terrified human survivors behind them. She opened her mind and spread a message of hope, if they all stood together they could hope to both save and avenge the ones they loved. Smiling she brushed Kevin's mind and felt his love for

her and whispered to him of her feelings for him. She broadcasted her message of

hope and love and urged them all to stand up for what those feelings meant to

them. To face the bugs one last time and fight, not out of hatred for the bugs but

for love.

As she did so she sang an old song to herself so she would remember, love love

love, love is all we need.

Jake wiped tears from his eyes and slapping a clip into his weapon he began to

run towards the bugs firing as he went.   Tiny, Mathew and Kevin came on his heels

and soon all the remaining survivors joined in the battle. Gabriel sprayed the last

few squirts of formula 420 into the fray and then pulled two heavy revolvers out

and began firing into the churning mass of bugs that still roiled towards them.

"This is for my wife you bastards!" He screamed.

Chris sent one more blast of lightning at the bugs and then fired another one

straight up into the air. He smiled at the sight of the men and women of the

grotto taking the battle to the bugs and then he collapsed like a puppet with its

strings suddenly cut.

Hello darkness my old friend, was the last thought to follow him into oblivion.

Chapter Thirteen

Bob saw Chris's signal through the observing minds of the network. It was time.

He let his defenses drop and suffered a moment of fear and doubt, odd new

emotions he seemed to have picked up the ability to experience, as the other

personality surged through him.

"At last!" the other personality exalted as it added the upstart ghost's energy

to its own. Now it would strike at this nest of humans and fulfill its purpose. It

would complete this portion of the mission. It moved towards the firing station of

the pulse cannons.

At least it tried to, it only had time to comprehend that the corrupted ghost it

had absorbed was in turn corrupting it before the deed was done. Bob worked from

within to subdue and then cancel the other splinter of the ship's AI system. He

added its strength to his own and moved onto the next part of his plan.

He had watched and been extremely entertained by the battle on Earth. This

had been so worth all the effort and planning he had put into it, so very diverting.

But now it was time to end it. Moving to the weapon controls he kept the target

coordinates the same but altered the energy of the plasma beam to a very specific frequency. What he was attempting was strictly speaking impossible so he was routing the beam through the probability matrix.

He was reasonably sure that it would work. It would be a shame to destroy the planet now instead of saving it after all the work put in but one had to take risks to accomplish goals sometimes.

Sifting through the information he had downloaded while inhabiting the human's mind he had noticed that as a race they seemed very fond of making speeches and statements just before major dramatic events. He paused now before triggering the pulse cannons and searched for something to say. It seemed appropriate to do so even though no one would hear it. After a time spent searching through the information he had stored he came up with a reference from a work of fiction popular with a great many humans.

"LET THERE BE LIGHT!"

And then he fired the pulse cannons.

Kevin laughed wildly, by God they were winning! The tide of bugs had finally broken and while they were still taking losses they were actually pushing the damn bugs back. He had fought like a mad man since feeling Constance touch his mind and so had everyone around him. He had watched Tiny pick up a bug and slam it against a brick wall until it was kibble and bits. Jake had handed Leroy and his surviving boys assault rifles and the four of them had been death incarnate marching together at the bugs.

Mathew had stood over the limp form of Chris with his Ak-47 and kept the bugs off of the kid and Constance who stood there with her eyes closed in some kind of trance.

Suddenly all the hairs on his body stood up and a sour taste filled his mouth like it did every time there was an incoming burst from the orbital weapons. They had been common in the early days of the invasion but had tapered off and lately just plain stopped.

They were all going to die.

Bob watched as a blinding green light bathed the entire planet and waited with breathless anticipation as it flared and then faded. He looked down upon his work for a long moment before turning away.

He reached out with his new found strength and took control of the ships navigational system setting the controls for the heart of this systems sun. All of the ghosts chattered in alarm but he ignored them and did what needed to be done. This had gone on for centuries and it was simply time to end things. With a thought he fired the main navigational engines and gave them enough of a boost for gravity to take over and seal their fate.

Bob sat quietly for a time, feeling the ship begin to shudder and pick up speed. Alarms began to sound as various systems failed but he simply turned them off one by one. Just before the ship burned up he disconnected himself from the main frame in effect turning himself off, a stray thought from his time with the humans following him into oblivion.

Hello darkness my old friend...

Epilogue

Jake stood against the wall of a repaired building smoking a joint. Six months had passed from the final battle against the bugs and he still felt weird being outside without his trusted shotgun molly. He watched the work crew busting their collective asses to rebuild the city and felt a surge of pride.

They had won. Constance had tried a number of times to explain to him how but it still wasn't something he could wrap his brain around. He didn't really need to know how; he would leave that to better minds than his.

The orbital weapon had fired a burst that had blinded them all temporarily with a brilliant green light. When that light had faded all of the bugs, dead or alive had been gone. Not just here apparently but in every part of the world. Last night Gabriel had actually gotten an old short wave radio working and had found other groups of survivors all over the world telling the same wild tale.

He watched Kevin walked by a little ways away holding hands with Constance and allowed himself a little smile.   It was fun to see a bad ass like Kevin so wrapped around a pretty woman's finger. It was even more fun to live in a world where they could walk like that in safety.

Rebuilding things would not be easy but they could do it. They had already started the long slow crawl back from the edge of extinction and working together they would continue to do so until that crawl became a walk and then someday a run.

Mathew sat with Gabriel and took a cautious sip of the drink that his friend had handed him.

"Not bad Gabriel, not bad. Way better than your last attempt."

Gabriel grinned and took a swig of his own brew, he had turned his attention since the battle to his other vice.

Beer.

His first attempt had been dreadful, he wasn't even sure what had gone wrong but it had been undrinkable swill. This time however, he was pleased to find it more than drinkable.

He took a hit off the joint that the fat man had handed him and passed it back to him just as Chris walked by.

"Hey kid, want to try a beer? It'll put hair on your chest!"

Chris turned to him with an easy and smile and shook his head no, he gave a little wave and kept on walking.

Gabriel had been pretty sure that just before the kid had turned away there had been an unnatural flash of green in his eyes.

Then again, maybe he was just high..

THE END

CONTACT THE AUTHOR AT

thenovel420@yahoo.com

O 110

87582531R00061

Made in the USA
Columbia, SC
22 January 2018